JULIE LAWSON
WERNER ZIMMERMANN

Whatever You Do, Don't Go Near That Canoe!

Scholastic Canada Ltd.

Toronto, New York, London, Sydney, Auckland

To Petra:

the memories of Tofino and Muskoka summer nights.

— W. Z.

For Stephanie.

— J. L.

Scholastic Canada Ltd.
123 Newkirk Road, Richmond Hill, Ontario, Canada L4C 3G5

Scholastic Inc.
555 Broadway, New York, NY 10012, USA

Scholastic Australia Pty Limited
PO Box 579, Gosford, NSW 2250, Australia

Scholastic New Zealand Limited
Private Bag 94407, Greenmount, Auckland, New Zealand

Scholastic Ltd.
Villiers House, Clarendon Avenue, Leamington Spa,
Warwickshire CV32 5PR, UK

This book was designed in Quark XPress,
with type set in 15 point Benguiat.

The illustrations were painted in watercolours
on Arches paper.

Canadian Cataloguing in Publication Data
Lawson, Julie, 1947-
Whatever you do, don't go near that canoe
ISBN 0-590-12422-6
I. Zimmermann, Werner. II. Title.
PS8573.A94W66 1998 jC813'.54 C97-931128-4
PZ7.L38Wh 1998

4 3 2   Printed in Canada   05 06 07
by Friesens

"Whatever you do, don't go near that canoe!"
Said Captain Kelsey McKee.
"Because if you do go near that canoe,
You'll have to reckon with me."

1

He winked as he spoke, and I thought to myself,
A challenge! What harm could there be?
So off we went — not too sure what he meant —
My brother, O'Malley, and me.

2

Through fast-running currents, through slow-rolling tides,
Far into the fading light,
Through sun flecks and sunset, through dusk's purple haze,
The canoe sped into the night.

"It's time to go back!" my brother exclaimed.
"It's time to be heading for home!"
But O'Malley knew, and I did, too —
That canoe had a mind of its own.

5

On the star side of morning a shadow appeared,
A finger of land loomed near;
And then, round the point, a sight met our eyes
That hammered our heartbeats with fear.

7

8

A pirate ship! with crossbones and skull
Snapping above the waves;
And there on the shore, five dozen or more
Piratical, seafaring knaves.

9

"Well shiver me timbers and scuttle me board!
This here is sure something to see!
Skuzzle me skullbones and frizzle me beard —
It's the dug-out of Captain McKee!

10

"Big Bart wants to know and he wants to know now,"
A pirate snarled into my face,
"How it is that you two got the Captain's canoe,
And how you discovered this place."

"Let's reel 'em and keel 'em," the pirates cried out.
"Let's teach 'em a lesson or two.
Let's splinter their giddles and twickle their toes,
For taking the Captain's canoe."

"O'Malley will come to our rescue," I said,
"She's totally fearless and tough."
But my brother exclaimed, "What the heck do you mean?
O'Malley is totally stuffed."

"Har, har!" roared the pirates. "Let's spangle their eyes!
Let's freakle their treacly hearts!"
Then a shuddering voice thundered low through the crowd:
"Let's give 'em a roast," growled Big Bart.

"Flare up the fire and flutter the flames!
Sharpen those sticks!" cried he.
"A relishing craving is coming my way
For the mateys of Captain McKee."

15

They led us up close to the crackling blaze
And shouted, "Get down on that log!"
Then they danced round the fire in riotous leaps,
While hollering "Flame-grill the dogs!"

16

17

I clasped my O'Malley, I closed my eyes tight,
I figured the end was near —
When my brother burst out, "What's that marvellous smell?
There's *marshmallows* roasting round here!"

"Sizzle me mallows!" Big Bart boomed,
Passing out wieners and buns,
"Roast a hot dog or two for your pet kangaroo —
There's plenty for everyone."

As the first glow of dawn shimmered over the sea
We feasted and drank ginger beer.
"A toast to our mates," sang the old salty dog.
"We're skin-tingling happy you're here."

20

Then he scooped up a handful of gleaming doubloons
And filled up my pet kangaroo.
"Take these to the Captain," he said with a grin,
"A present from Bart and the crew."

23

Through the rippling water the dug-out sped home,
Straight into the Captain's arms.
"It worked!" he exclaimed, with a cartwheeling flip,
"My invention — it worked like a charm!"

He tied the canoe, then he counted the coins,
While praising Big Bart to the skies.
"What a fine buccaneer! What a piratey treat!"
And "Oh! What a splendid surprise!"

But he bit into chocolate when testing the gold,
So the trick was on him, in the end.
"Well, whistle me whiskers! That rascally rogue
Has royally foiled me again."

We ate the gold coins and thanked Captain McKee
For his wizardly wonderful trip.
"Not at all!" he replied. "Awfully glad to oblige!
But I'll give you just one little tip . . .

"You kids stay away from my twin-engined sleigh —
I'm not fooling this time, no sirree."
And then, with a twinkle, he said "Adios!"
To my brother, O'Malley, and me.

28